Sindbad

IN THE LAND OF GIANTS

Sindbad

IN THE LAND OF GIANTS

Retold and Illustrated by Ludmila Zeman

Tundra Books

Published in Canada by Tundra Books, *McClelland & Stewart Young Readers*,
481 University Avenue, Toronto, Ontario M5G 2E9

Published in the United States by Tundra Books of Northern New York,
P.O. Box 1030, Plattsburgh, New York 12901

Library of Congress Control Number: 00-131581

Canadian Cataloguing in Publication Data

Zeman, Ludmila
  Sindbad in the land of giants

ISBN 0-88776-461-4

I. Title.

PS8599.E492S564 2001   jC813'.54   C00-932277-9
PZ7.Z417Si 2001

We acknowledge the support of the Canada Council for the Arts and the Ontario Arts Council for our publishing program.

We acknowledge the financial support of the Government of Canada through the Book Publishing Industry Development Program for our publishing activities.

Design: Sari Naworynski

Medium: pencil, colored pencil, and watercolor on paper

Printed in Hong Kong, China

1 2 3 4 5 6   06 05 04 03 02 01

I wish to thank my daughter Linda Spaleny,
who has patiently helped and encouraged me in creating this book.

The morning sun woke ancient Baghdad. Its rays glittered on the golden rooftops, and melodic prayers resounded from slim minarets. In the most exquisite palace, poor Sindbad the Porter felt soft silk brush against his shoulder as the smell of fresh-brewed tea roused him from a sweet dream. Yet the palace was no dream. Sindbad the Porter had been summoned here three days earlier by Sindbad the Sailor to listen to tales of wondrous travels filled with danger and excitement. The porter never imagined that a man of such wealth could have endured so much toil and hardship.

Sindbad the Sailor rested comfortably on satin pillows, sipping his cup of tea. "Today, humble Porter, I will tell you a story even more incredible than the one I told you yesterday:

I was on a merchant ship returning to Baghdad. I had diamonds in my pocket and thought of nothing else but resuming my life in the city, never again to set foot on the deck of another ship. But soon enough my desire for city life grew distant, and passion for the sea and trading once again enslaved me. I persuaded some fellow merchants to take me with them to foreign lands.

For months we drifted on the ocean. One morning at the break of dawn, the captain of the ship pointed, with trembling hand, at the dark mountain on the far horizon. He cried out in terror: 'O wise merchants, save yourselves! We have been driven off course by the cruel winds. We are headed for the treacherous Mountain of the Monkeys.'

We tried to steer our ship away from the peninsula, but all was in vain. As we came close to shore, creatures with black hairy coats and small yellow eyes jumped onboard, taunting all the merchants and sailors. We allowed them to ransack our ship, gnawing the ropes and cables to bits. We feared that if we hurt one of the scoundrels, the rest would surely kill us.

Desperation drove some of the merchants overboard — they jumped into the waves in sheer terror. The rest of us tried to keep our wits about us. We made our way through the monkeys to the starboard side of the ship, where a small boat was attached. Beneath the veil of darkness, we quietly pushed off and headed straight for the peninsula. The remains of our ship swayed precariously, with hundreds of monkeys onboard.

When we reached the shore, we set out to explore the mountain. Miraculously we spotted what appeared to be an inhabited castle. We climbed towards it as fast as our feet could carry us, with fresh hope in our hearts. Our spirits sank when we saw that the entrance to the magnificent castle was garnished with human bones.

efore we could advance any farther, the earth trembled and a huge manlike beast glared at us. His eyes were balls of fire and his mouth, as wide as a lake. He lowered his clawed hands and lifted us in the air. He carried us into his castle and, like little chickens, stuffed us into a bamboo birdcage.

Some of the merchants managed to escape. As they ran desperately for the gate, the giant lifted them up again and tore them to pieces.

I was horrified at the thought of perishing in the beast's belly. Suddenly, dying in combat with a pierced heart or drowning beneath fierce ocean waves seemed rather appealing.

For supper the giant merrily grilled our captain and seasoned him with exotic herbs to add flavor to his bland taste. Since the captain had hardly been a slim man, the beast filled up quickly and fell asleep.

We loosened a few bamboo rods so that we could climb up to the window. By running from one side of the cage to the other, we swung the cage close enough for one of the merchants to grab a bamboo rod and climb out onto the window ledge.

Suddenly, the beast awoke. With an enormous roar he ran towards us. The cage swung back and, like two large swords, the bamboo rods flew right into the giant's eyes.

The beast roared in anguish. He wanted to stop us from running away, but he could not see. In rage he smashed everything around him until the castle started to crumble. Quickly, we ran towards the boat and set out on the ocean, paddling as fast as we could away from that treacherous land.

Suddenly, a shower of large stones rained from the sky. When the other giants heard their brother's roar and saw what we had done, they were determined to kill us. But they did not see our little boat, hidden by the raging waters. They began to throw huge boulders at the ship until, with all the monkeys, it disappeared beneath the waves.

Only one merchant and I managed to save ourselves. We had been swimming for days when I realized that if we did not reach land that morning, we would surely die.

As fate would have it, the most unusual island appeared on the horizon. Its trees were magnificent and gave off a beautiful scent. We kicked our feet in the waves, trying to propel our boat ahead as quickly as possible, happy that the island looked deserted.

As soon as we stepped onshore, however, a beast with one large horn in

place of its nose came running towards us at incredible speed. With no time to rest for even a moment, we were forced to run towards a wild river, where another friendly creature with razor-sharp teeth greeted us with wide-open jaws. Our fear seemed to attach springs to our feet and we propelled ourselves up, grabbing a tree branch. The creature did not count on such a large morsel as the horned beast, and floated happily back into the river. My merchant friend and I stayed suspended from the branch until evening, shaking so violently that nearly all the leaves fell off the tree.

Realizing that we were still alive, we decided to climb to the treetop to spend the night. As I fell asleep, I heard a hissing sound very close to my ear. Opening my eyes, I beheld a snake the size of a dragon. At first I thought I was dreaming (because surely, a snake of that size could not exist), but to my amazement my companion disappeared instantly in the snake's giant mouth. The serpent swallowed him whole and slithered back into the forest.

Terrified that the snake would return for me for dessert, I quickly climbed down the tree and began collecting dry pieces of wood, binding them together with lianas to make a raft.

Sure enough, the snake returned at nightfall.

I hid among the roots of the tree, so deformed that they created a perfect cage. The snake tried to get to me all night and I prayed that my shelter would endure. When the morning sun cast its rays, the serpent departed in fury. I freed myself from the entangled roots and quickly finished my raft.

Placing my primitive vessel in the water, I drifted downriver. I had no idea where I was headed. The river was calm, but many wild creatures encircled me. Fearing that I would fall off, I tied myself to the raft and soon fell asleep.

The noise of falling rocks woke me. I held on to the raft with all my strength and thought: *Why did I ever set out on another voyage? If I ever come out of this alive, I will never travel again.*

Next thing I remember, I heard human voices above me. Foreign men were fishing me out of the water. They threatened to kill me for invading their land. 'Please wait,' I pleaded. 'First let me tell you my story.'

They were so amazed by my fantastic tale that they immediately summoned their scribes to transcribe it as an incredible voyage of a man who must be more than a mere mortal. They promised to grant me anything I wished in exchange for such a story. 'Give me a ship to take me to Baghdad,' I asked. And they did....

But, curiously, there was much more to come. After I rest I will tell you about my last voyage, which convinced me to return to Baghdad forever and never to venture on the ocean again."

Author's Note

Shahrazad's voice was like music as she spoke to the king:
"Do not go to bed, Sire, for I have a tale to tell."

The king was a wicked man who used to take a new wife every night, only to order her beheaded at dawn. Shahrazad was a brave woman who offered to be the king's wife, to put an end to his wicked ways. When night fell, Shahrazad began to weave a story. She was but halfway through when morning came. The king needed rest and whispered, "Finish the tale when I awake." That night, Shahrazad finished her story and immediately began another, even more enticing than the first. And so it went for a thousand and one nights, until the king forgot his wicked ways.

Shahrazad enthralled the king with stories that became known as the *Thousand and One Nights,* or *Arabian Nights.* Through vivid storytelling of now famous tales, such as *Aladdin, Ali Baba and the Forty Thieves,* or *Sindbad the Sailor,* Shahrazad not only saved her life, but also cured the king of hatred and fear. In *Sindbad in the Land of Giants,* Sindbad the Sailor follows her example and manages to save his own life by a colorful and magical description of his adventures to the strangers that apprehend him. I tried to pursue the same road by visually retelling one of the most extraordinary of the thousand and one stories.

The story of Sindbad is not only steeped in wisdom, but also demonstrates the value of other cultures in today's global society. Sindbad and his overseas trading allowed me to show children distant oceans, wondrous regions of the Middle East and Southeast Asia, and incredible monuments like the great temple at Angkor — in today's Cambodia — that is continually admired as a world masterpiece.